K and the Ultimate Thumb-Wrestling Smackdown

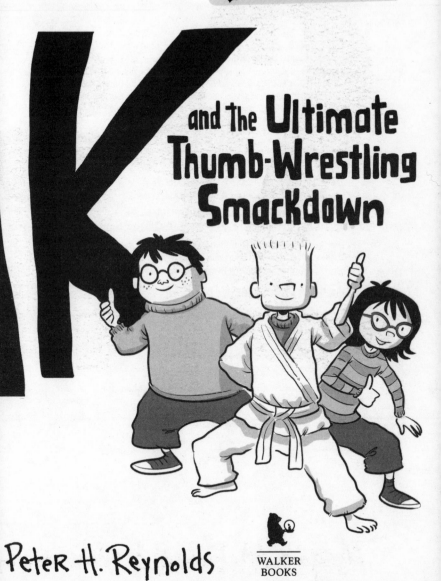

Peter H. Reynolds

WALKER
BOOKS

First published 2011 by Walker Books Ltd
87 Vauxhall Walk, London SE11 5HJ

2 4 6 8 10 9 7 5 3 1

Text © 2011 Megan McDonald
Illustrations © 2011 Peter H. Reynolds

Stink ™. Stink is a registered trademark of
Candlewick Press, Inc, Somerville MA

The right of Megan McDonald and Peter H. Reynolds to be identified as author and illustrator respectively of this work has been asserted by them in accordance with the Copyright, Designs and Patents Act 1988

This book has been typeset in Stone Informal

Printed in Great Britain by Clays Ltd, St Ives plc

British Library Cataloguing in Publication Data:
a catalogue record for this book is available from the British Library

ISBN 978-1-4063-3458-6

www.stinkmoody.com

www.walker.co.uk

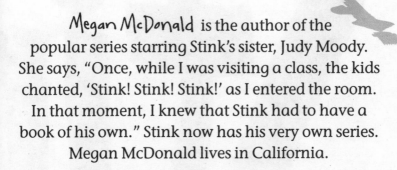

Megan McDonald is the author of the
popular series starring Stink's sister, Judy Moody.
She says, "Once, while I was visiting a class, the kids
chanted, 'Stink! Stink! Stink!' as I entered the room.
In that moment, I knew that Stink had to have a
book of his own." Stink now has his very own series.
Megan McDonald lives in California.

You can find out more about Megan McDonald
and her books at **www.meganmcdonald.net**

Peter H. Reynolds is the illustrator of all
the Judy Moody and Stink books. He says, "Stink
reminds me of myself growing up: dealing with a
sister prone to teasing and bossing around – and
having to get creative in order to stand tall beside
her." Peter H. Reynolds lives in Massachusetts.

You can find out more about Peter H. Reynolds
and his art at **www.fablevision.com**

Stin

Megan McDonald illustrated by

for Nathan and Eric
M. M.

for Rocky
P. H. R.

CONTENTS

Crackdown!

Smackdown!

Thwackdown!

Stink stared at the stack of super-secret sealed envelopes on Mrs D.'s desk. He could hardly wait.

Report Card Day!

Report Card Day was the best day ever in the whole entire school year. Right after Crazy Hat Day and Pyjama Day, that is.

At last it was time. Mrs D. handed

him an envelope. A brand-spanking-new envelope with a shiny little window that said: TO THE PARENTS OF JAMES E. MOODY.

Stink took a sniff. Stink took a whiff. He could almost smell the perfect ink used to write down all the good grades he was about to get.

"Remember," said Mrs D., "no opening until you have a parent present."

Just then, the bell rang. Stink put the envelope in his Wednesday folder. He put the folder in his backpack. He rushed out the door.

On the bus, Stink could not stand it one more minute. He took out the super-secret sealed envelope.

"You better not open it," said his best friend Webster.

"You better not open it," said his other best friend, Sophie of the Elves.

"I'm just looking," said Stink.

"Stink, put that away," said his sister, Judy. "You're not allowed to open it till we get home."

Stink held the envelope to the light. He pressed it against the bus window.

"O, O, O, O, O," said Stink. "I see a lot of O's for *Outstanding*!"

"Zeros," said Judy, cracking up. "You got all zeros."

"Hardee-har-har," said Stink.

Stink had ants in his pants all the way home. Bees in his knees. Flies in his eyes. Stink felt like a hopping popcorn kernel just about to p-o-p!

Stink raced into the house.

He took out his Wednesday folder and handed the envelope to Mum. "Open it, open it, open it."

"Let's wait for Dad."

"But the sooner you open it," said Stink, "the sooner we can hang it on the fridge in the Moody Hall of Fame. I know I got all O's."

"O is for *oh, brother*," Judy said.

✳   ✳   ✳

Report card time!

Dad peered over Mum's shoulder. They smiled proud smiles for all the big fat cheery O's on his report card.

"Good for you, honey," said Mum, putting an arm around him.

"Lots of *Outstandings*. You should be proud of yourself, Stink," said Dad.

"Aren't you going to hang it on the fridge now?" Stink asked. "In the Moody Hall of Fame? Above Judy's?"

Mum and Dad didn't answer. Mum and Dad stared at the report card. Mum and Dad read the comments at the bottom.

All of a sudden, their smiles turned into straight lines. The straight lines turned into upside-down smiles. Mum and Dad were frowning!

"What's this?" asked Dad, pointing to the bottom of the report card.

"Seems to be a *U*," said Mum.

U! U was for *Ucky*! U was for *U stink*! U was for … *Unless You're an O, What Are You Doing on My Report Card?*

"Stink got a U?" Judy asked. "U is for *UN-satisfactory*! U is for *U flunked*!"

"In Phys Ed," said Dad.

"Fizz Ed?" Stink asked. "Who's Ed?"

"Phys Ed," said Mum. "Physical Education."

"Gym," said Judy. "You know, like sports."

"Sports? I like sports," said Stink.

"Driving your race-car bed is not a sport," said Judy.

"I like basketball."

"Which you play in your room while sitting on your UN-sports race-car bed."

"I like baseball too. And football."

"You like collecting baseball cards and watching the Steelers on TV with Dad. Waving the Terrible Towel around? Also not a sport."

"Can I help it if I'm short and can't reach the basket? Can I help it if the bat's bigger than me? Can I help it if I get crushed in American football? Do you want a brother who's flat as a pancake?"

"Silver-dollar or blueberry?" Judy asked.

"Mum and I would still like you to take up a sport," said Dad.

"Just because of one puny U, I have

to get crushed like a pancake?"

"There are plenty of sports you can play. I was short like you, but I was the fastest kid on the Roanoke Racerbacks."

"All kids need exercise. And fresh air," said Mum. "It'll be fun."

"What about Judy? Doesn't she have to play a sport?"

"Hello! I play football. And softball. And I do swim team in the summer."

"Playing a sport will really help you bring this grade up," said Dad.

Stink's lip quivered like wiggly spaghetti.

"In sports, you get to wear a cool uniform," said Judy. "And bring home a shiny trophy. And go to a pizza party at the end of the season."

Stink looked at Mum and Dad. Stink looked at Judy. But instead of eyes, all he could see were U's.

The next day, Stink went looking for a sport.

Webster liked bike-riding and basketball. Sophie of the Elves liked ballet, gymnastics and African dance. Skunk liked skateboarding.

But Stink's bike had a flat tyre. He had two left feet. And the only skateboard he owned was the one without wheels hanging on his wall.

Then Stink checked out the sports channels. He watched slow-pitch

softball (BOR-ing), golf (WAY-boring),
badminton (Stink was no-way, NOT
going to hit a bird) and stuff where
guys called each other goofy names
like Steve-a-rino and Pa Jammy.

Stink watched ditch-snorkelling (too

muddy!), tuna-throwing (Mum did NOT like him to throw stuff), Tootsie-Roll spitting (Mum did NOT like him to spit stuff, either), cheese-chasing (huh?) and wife-carrying (Hel-*lo*! Stink did NOT have a wife!).

Stink was just about to give up when he heard the words "most fun classic sport ever". Then he heard, "Play it at home! In the car! At school! Free! No equipment necessary!"

Stink was glued to the screen. "Hey, sports fans! Have we got the sport for you! It's fab. It's free. It's fun-tastic! Strength. Stamina. Strategy. Two thumbs up for the sport that's sweeping the nation – thumb-wrestling!"

Thumb-wrestling was *uber*-cool. Thumb-wrestling was F-U-N! Thumb-wrestling was *thumb*-tastic!

Stink watched three thumb-wrestling

matches in a row. He learned the rules. Easy peasy! He practised on himself. Best of all, he learned tricky moves with funny names like Snake in the Grass and Santa's Little Helper.

All he needed now was someone to thumb-wrestle… Webster!

✷ ✷ ✷

"One, two, three, four, I declare a thumb war!"

Stink wrinkled his forehead. Stink stuck out his tongue. Stink made funny faces. Stink and Webster's thumbs were locked in a bitter battle.

Webster tried to pin Stink's thumb

down one, two, three times, but Stink escaped in the nick of time.

Webster waited. Webster barely blinked. Webster looked sneaky. "Gotcha!" Webster chortled with glee, smashing his thumb down over Stink's and trapping it for three seconds.

"You win," said Stink. "Again."

"Yes!" Webster pumped his fist in the air. "I'm mucho macho!"

"No fair. Your thumb's longer than mine," said Stink.

"Is not," said Webster. They held up their thumbs side by side. "See? They're *almost* the same."

"I'm left-handed," said Stink. "Try again. This time we do it lefty."

They went at it again, left-handed. Left-*thumbed,* that is. Stink tried to trick Webster. But it was no use. Even left-handed, Webster chewed him up and spat him out like yesterday's breakfast cereal.

"Stink, you're all thumbs today."
Webster cracked up.

"Hardee-har-har," said Stink.

"I'm the best *luchador* this side of
Chuckamuck Creek."

"The best what?" Stink asked.

"*Luchador.* It means *wrestler* in
Spanish. My dad was a wrestler in
high school, and my two uncles."

They played again. And again.
Webster beat Stink every time. "I stink
at thumb-wrestling," said Stink.

"So? You *don't* stink at catching toads.
And you don't stink at rescuing guinea
pigs and saving Pluto. And smelling."

31

"Great. I smell. Told you I stink."

Webster hee-hawed. "But you've never played before. Stick with it."

"Hold the phone!" said Stink. "Let's make masks, for our thumbs. Like they wear on smackdown wrestling. We can give them scary faces, so they look bad. Real bad."

"The baddest," said Webster.

Stink got out scissors, felt, glue, markers and a bag of googly eyes. "Mine's gonna be green, with a black Batman mask for eyes and red flames on top," said Webster.

"Mine's gonna be silver with pointy

red teeth and a black shark fin on top."

"We SO don't stink at this," said Webster, grinning.

Done. Webster and Stink slipped the masks over their thumbs.

"Cool," said Webster.

"Bad," said Stink.

"Dweebs," said Stink's sister, Judy, coming into the room. "Why are you guys making finger puppets? Finger puppets are for babies."

"They're not finger puppets," said Stink.

"They're *luchadores*," said Webster. "Like pro wrestlers from Mexico. Now we have to think up names for them."

"How about El Terrible and El Even Worso?" Judy cracked herself up.

Stink ignored her.

"Tweedle Thumb and Tweedle Dumb?" Judy suggested.

Webster held up his thumb mask. "Meet … T. Rex Wasabi."

"Presenting … Shark Hammersmash," said Stink. "T. Rex Wasabi and Shark Hammersmash are warming up for the big event: the Ultimate Thumb-Wrestling *Thmack*down."

Webster didn't miss a beat. "T. Rex Wasabi is favoured to win 7–1. But underdog Shark Hammersmash could come from behind with a sneak attack. You might say he's a Snake in the Grass. A little Bug in the Ear."

"You might say he's a little *Pain* in the *Rear*," said Judy, grinning.

"Please?" Stink begged. "Pretty please with Screamin' Mimi's ice cream on top?"

"Forget it. I'm not going to thumb-wrestle. Mum and Dad said you have to play a *sport*."

"Thumb-wrestling is on the sports channel. Thumb-wrestling has all three S's: Strength, stamina and strategy."

"Do you even know what that means?" Judy asked.

"Hel-*lo*! I read the S encyclopedia."

"Trust me, Stink. Mum and Dad are not going to go for thumb-wrestling."

"That's why I have to wow them with my amazing skill. For serious. If I practise a bunch, I can win the Ultimate Thumb-Wrestling Thmackdown."

"Thorry," Judy teased. "I have homework." She bounced a bouncy ball off the wall.

"Homework? You're just bouncing a ball."

"I'm counting how many times I can bounce it off the wall – 107, 108, 109 – without dropping it. Like a science experiment."

"Your science experiment could be to see how many times you can beat your little brother at thumb-wrestling."

"Stink. You're wrecking my concentration," said Judy.

Stink did not stop talking. "Did you know that thumb-wrestling goes way-way way back to the time of the Romans?"

"Uh-huh. 110, 111, 112, 113."

"Back then, they thumb-wrestled

in a big stadium. Bazillions of people came to watch."

"Uh-huh." 114, 115, 116.

"And they thumb-wrestled *to the* death."

Judy stopped bouncing the ball. "That is SO not true. People don't die from thumb-wrestling."

"They wrestled to the death … of the thumb. You were the loser when your thumbnail turned all black and gross and fell off. Then the winner took the gross thumbnail and ran around the arena with it. The crowds went wild and yelled, 'All hail the thumbnail.'"

"Stink, you lie like a guy with a booger in his eye."

"Nah-uh. I swear." He held up his left thumb. "Thumb-wrestler's honour. Now that you know how cool and gross it is, will you thumb-wrestle me?"

"Still no."

"Not even if I give you my Liberty Bell postcard and my Ocean Breeze Water Park squished penny?"

"You've got to come up with something better than that, Stink."

"I promise not to put my smelly feet on you for one whole entire week."

"Tempting," said Judy. She flung the

ball against the wall extra hard.

"Never mind. I'm stronger anyway."

"Are not," said Judy.

"Am too," said Stink.

"Are not."

"Prove it," said Stink. "Prove it like Nancy Drew."

"OK, I give up. But remember, I'm up to 128." Judy set the ball down.

Stink put on Shark Hammersmash. Judy drew a way-moody mood face on her thumbnail. "Shark Hammersmash, meet Manta Ray Moody."

Judy and Stink locked fingers. "May the best thumb win," said Judy.

"One, two, three, four, I declare a thumb war!" In two seconds flat, Judy had crushed Stink's thumb with her index finger. "I win!" she shouted.

"No fair! Fingers are against the law. The first Rule of Thumb is no snakes, bugs, trapdoors or sidekicks. And definitely NO Santa's Little Helper."

"Huh?"

"No sneak attacks from fingers. Just thumbs."

"Fine. But you're goin' down, Shark Hammersmash. You're goin' down so far, your undies will be dragging in the dirt."

Stink ducked his thumb.

"The Manta Ray is gonna crush you like ice, Shark. You're a snow cone."

"I am not a snow cone. Stop saying stuff."

Judy pointed out the window. "Look! Halley's Comet!"

"You just want me to look away so you can body slam me."

"Busted," said Judy. "But there IS a giant jawbreaker on the bookcase. No, wait. It's a moon rock! You gotta see it, Stink."

"Later." He dipped his thumb one, two, three times.

"Yeti alert! Behind you. Very big, very hairy yeti! No lie."

Yeti? Stink turned to look.

"Gotcha!" said Judy. "One, two, three. Smackdown! I pinned you for three counts. I win. Take that, Shark Hammersmash."

"But you made me look."

"So? It's not my fault that you fell for the old Yeti trick. Manta Ray Moody rules! Shark Hammersmash is mincemeat. Shark Hammersmash is chopped liver."

"Shark Hammersmash is ripped! Look what you did. He lost one eye."

"Told you. Never tangle with the Moodinator."

Judy drew stitches like a Frankenstein scar on Stink's mask. Then she wrapped a pirate Band-Aid around its head. And she gave him a black eye where his googly eye used to be.

"Now he looks way tougher. He's been knocked out a few times, but he has cool scars to show for it."

"*Franken*shark Hammersmash," said Stink, grinning from ear to ear.

GRRR!

SHARK
HAMMERSMASH
VS
T. REX WASABI

RAR!

Sneak attack!

Hey Cheaterpants! No fingers!

That's called a Snake in the Grass!

I call it the Trap Door.

You mean Santa's Little Helper?

I don't care if it's the Tooth Fairy.

It's still cheating!

On the bus, Shark Hammersmash thumb-wrestled Rocky and Frank. In the boys' room, Shark Hammersmash thumb-wrestled Skunk. The Shark went down one, two, three times.

At morning break, at lunch and in the playground, Shark Hammersmash thumb-wrestled Riley Rottenberger (still rotten), Heather Strong (who really *was* strong) and some first-grader named Johnson Splink (no lie). The Shark took a beating every time.

In class, Mrs D. was teaching about money. Dollars and cents. Quarters, dimes and nickels. She passed around trays of fake paper money and plastic coins.

"Pair up with your partner and help each other give correct change. I'll be in the hall hanging artwork. So I'm going to turn on the Yack Buster Deluxe."

Not the Yack Buster Deluxe! The Yack Buster Deluxe 6XM was a stop-light in the corner of the room. When Class 2D kept their voices low, the light stayed green. If they started to get noisy, the light turned yellow. If they got way too noisy, the stoplight turned red. In the deluxe model, a siren even went off.

Stink Moody did NOT have a good track record with the Yack Buster Deluxe 6XM. Once he'd dropped his maths book and the siren had gone off.

Another time he fell off his chair and the siren went cuckoo. *Woo-oo-woo!*

Mrs D. turned on the machine. The green light blinked. The red light was not lit up, but it stared at Stink like a black eye waiting to happen.

As soon as Mrs D. left the room, Stink said to Sophie, "Let's thumb-wrestle."

"Thumb-wrestle? I don't know how."

Thunderation! The Shark had found his bait. Stink would beat the pants off Sophie in a mini smackdown. *No problemo!*

"I'll show you," said Stink.

"In the middle of maths class?"

"It only takes two seconds." *Two seconds to crush you*, Stink thought.

Stink taught Sophie how to lock hands. Stink taught Sophie the rules. Stink taught Sophie to say, "One, two, three, four, I declare a thumb war!"

"I don't like war games."

"It's not *really* war," said Stink. "It's wrestling. Think of it like a sport."

"Then why did you say war?"

"It rhymes with *four*," said Stink.

"*S'more* rhymes with *four*," said Sophie. "One, two, three, four, I declare a thumb s'more!"

The S'more Showdown began.

Stink thumb-wrestled with all his might, but Sophie pinned him flat for three counts in no time. He was a s'more, all right. A smushed-flat marshmallow.

"Go again," said Stink. Stink bit his tongue. Stink tried not to think of s'mores.

Class 2D forgot all about the Yack Buster Deluxe 6XM.

"Smash her down, Shark!" yelled the boys.

"Watch out for the Marshmallowizer!" said the girls.

Sophie took Stink down again. "Just call me Sophie of the Thumbs."

"Best out of three?" Stink asked.

Nobody was doing maths. Nobody was counting fake money. The room got loud. The room got louder.

"Get the butter – you're toast!" yelled the boys.

"Prepare to die, Shark Hammer-smash!" the girls yelled back.

The Yack Buster's yellow light came on, blazing bright as the sun. Nobody noticed. The Yack Buster's red light came on. Nobody stopped.

Woo-oo-woo! The Yack Buster's siren went off, louder than a smoke alarm. Louder than a fire engine. "Make it stop!" Stink yelled. "Before we get into mucho trouble!"

Stink raced over to the Yack Buster. He could not find the off button.

Woo-oo-woo! Woo-oo-woo! Stink threw the reading quilt over it.

Mrs D. rushed into the room. "What in the world?" She ran to her desk, grabbed the remote and pushed buttons. Ahh. Quiet.

Mrs D. put her hands on her hips. Mrs D. made her serious teacher face. Mrs D. said I'm-not-happy words.

"Somebody must have dropped a maths book," said Webster.

"Or knocked over the bin," said Skunk.

Heather Strong pointed at Stink. "Stink Moody was thumb-wrestling!"

Before you could say Ultimate After-School Thmackdown, Stink was out in the hall with Mrs D. Tomorrow, Stink would not be thumb-wrestling at school. Stink would be picking up litter on the playground at playtime.

And he had to take a not-happy note home to his parents.

A note from the teacher was worse than a U on his report card. A note from the teacher was UN-satisfactory! A note from the teacher meant only one thing: IN BIG TROUBLE.

SMART MOVES FOR VICTORY

THE HEAD-BUTT

BOK!

Two thumbs go head-to-head. When one thumb tires and slips - quick! Trap him!

PLAYING POSSUM

Thumb acts dead and doesn't make a move. Suddenly - Cobra Strike!

HALLEY'S COMET

Look! Halley's Comet!

Huh?

Distract your opponent. Point and yell, "Look! Halley's Comet!"

"Did Mum and Dad read the note? Are you in trouble?" Judy asked Stink.

"I won't be seeing my allowance till I'm a teenager," said Stink. "AND I have to think up a new sport."

Stink ran up to his room. "This is not the end of Shark Hammersmash," he whispered to his thumb mask.

No fair! Stink was pencil-snapping mad. He slammed his hand fist-down on his desk. Yikes. He'd snapped a pencil right in half.

Stink did not know his own *strength*! Stink had the *stamina* to snap more pencils. Suddenly, Stink felt like punching stuff. Stink felt like kicking stuff. Stink felt like chopping stuff with his bare hands. Stink had a new *strategy* – he, Stink E. Moody, would be the new karate kid!

So what if he did not have a karate uniform? He pulled on his blue bathrobe. He wrapped the belt around his waist (twice) and tied it in a knot. Presto! Stink was already a blue belt.

Ka-pow! Stink threw a vertical punch. *Kee-yah!* Trading cards went flying off the mirror. *Ka-poom!* He kicked his sand-dollar collection off the shelf. Stink pulled back his elbow and *wham!* He knocked out the Hulk, Iron Man, Wolverine, Sabretooth and all four of the Fantastic Four.

Stink karate-kicked the air. *Ha-cha!* His cardboard guitar fell off the wall. *Yee-ah!* His lava lamp almost tipped over. *Youch.* One kick to the wall, and he ripped his original *Star Wars* poster and his Super Reading Award certificate.

There just wasn't enough room for a super high-flying ultra-death-defying karate kick. Stink ran across the hall to Judy's room. He stuck one leg out and gave a super-duper, mile-high-flying foot-jab way up in the air. *BANZAI!*

Uh-oh. Something fell and crashed to the floor. *E-I-E-I-O!* Judy's trophy! Her Giraffe Award – the third-grade prize she'd won for sticking her neck out for others – had just become the Headless Giraffe Award.

Stink duck-taped it back together. Good as new! Almost. He hid the now-wobbly, bobble-headed Giraffe Award behind some piles of Nancy Drew books.

He ran downstairs to tell Mum and Dad all about his new sport. Mum said karate was right up Stink's alley. Dad went online and signed him up for a class!

Stink could not wait to get started. In the living room, he karate-chopped the encyclopedia. *Youch!* In the kitchen, he karate-chopped spaghetti, pretzel sticks and a box of cereal. Mood Flakes flew across the floor. In the TV room, he spied Judy's lost-and-found pencil collection sitting on a shelf. Perfect!

U-na-gi! With each karate chop, another pencil went zinging through the air. Smiley-face pencils, Student-of-the-Week pencils, Virginia Dare School pencils.

"Stink!" Judy yelled at her pencil-snapping, cuckoo-head brother.

"So what? These are just loser pencils you found on the floor at school."

"I'm collecting them. To show the head teacher how many pencils are wasted."

Stink held up his hand. "Don't talk to me. Talk to The Hand. This bad boy is a human chopping machine. It can't stop. It has to chop."

"Here. You can chop my Attitude is Everything pencil. But that's all."

Stink raised his hand. Mouse dashed under the sofa. Stink karate-chopped the pencil. Now it said TUDE IS EVERYTHING.

"Fear The Hand." The Hand sliced the air. "You'd better be way nice to me now. I'll be able to grab you by the hair and flip you upside-down."

"Ha. I don't think so."

"It's ka-rah-tay. My new sport. By next week, this bad boy will be chopping through cement blocks." *Chop-chop-chop-chop-chop.* "Just call me *Chop*zilla."

Chopzilla karate-chopped a sofa cushion. Feathers went flying. The room became a whirling, swirling snowstorm of white feathers. Snow-globe city!

Mouse streaked through the snow-storm and out of the room.

"Pff." Judy tried to talk, but only a feather came out. "Mum's gonna freak. It looks like you wrestled the Abominable Snowman. I'm going to my room."

"Don't go upstairs!" Stink yelled, following her up the steps.

"Stink? What did you do?" Judy looked all around her room. "Why do you keep staring at my Nancy Drew books?" She rushed over to the shelf. "STINK! You broke my Giraffe Award? This is one-of-a-kind!"

"Please don't be mad. I'll glue all the loser pencils back together, and I'll help pick up pencils after school for the rest of the year."

"OK."

"OK? For real?"

"OK. You can help me pick up pencils after school."

"I will. I swear. Itchy kata's honour. I'll help. Every day. Except Tuesdays and Thursdays and every other Friday, because that's karate."

TRADING CARDS

He's big! He's bad!
Back from the grave,
he's the mummy of all
thumb wrestlers.
Favoured to win,
of _corpse_!

☆ THUMMY ☆

Calm? Cool? Collected?
Ha! The Dragon is out to
destroy the mummy.
He's a hundred-degree
— hothead. —
☰ Warning ☰
Don't Fight Fire with fire!

☆ DRAGON MASTER ☆

He's red. He's loud.
This rooster's up at dawn,
practising his moves. Is he
all strut and no stuff?
Has his _cluck_ just run out?

RAGIN'
☆ ROOSTER RAMSICLE ☆

He shivers. He quivers.
He hides in the
corner.
Will he shed his blankie
and face the Thummy?
Or will he run crying
to his mummy?

THUMB-SUCKER
AKA
☆ BINKY BOO-HOO ☆

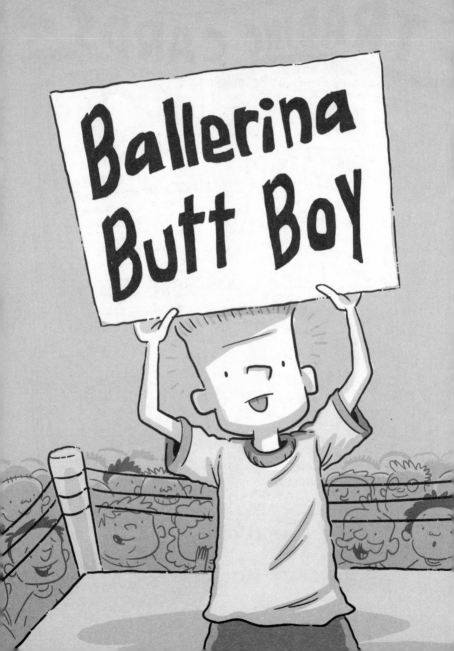

"Welcome to Empty Hand Academy," said a girl with a yin-yang headband. "I'm Izzy. I'm an orange belt, so I help new kids."

Stink breathed it all in. One whole wall was a mirror. Black-and-orange training mats covered the floor. Foam-covered punching bags stood guard in the corner. On the wall were the words: RESPECT. CONFIDENCE. FOCUS. SELF-DEFENCE. BETTER GRADES.

"Take off your shoes," said Izzy. Stink kicked off his smelly sneakers. He stepped on to the mat in his sock feet. His feet went flying.

Izzy laughed. "You just learned your first move: the Flying Butt Fall."

"I see our new student is off to a flying start," joked a guy with shaggy hair and a black belt. Stink picked himself up.

"Stink Moody," said Izzy, "this is our teacher, Mr Albion. We call him Sensei Dan."

Sensei Dan bowed to Stink. "Hello. Welcome. Take off your socks, Stink

Moody. In karate, we have more control in bare feet."

"Who's that?" Stink asked, pointing to a life-size cardboard action figure of a guy doing karate.

"That's the Venerable Yuuto Kashiwagi," Izzy answered. "He's a world-famous karate champ. We call him Dragon Master."

"Warm-ups, everybody," Mr Albion called. Kids walked around the edges of the mat.

"I am only I," said Sensei Dan.

"I am only I," the class repeated.

"I walk in my own footsteps."

"I walk in my own footsteps," said the class.

Next, they sat on the floor and did push-ups, crunches and stretches. Then they crossed their legs, closed their eyes and focused on a calming image.

Stink opened his eyes. Stink did not feel calm. All he could think about was karate-kicking – *hi-ya* – and punching – *ka-pow* – and chop-o-matic chopping. Where were all the boards for chopping? *Ai-ee!*

"Let's try not to make sound effects during the calming meditation," said Sensei Dan.

Stink turned cherry-red.

"Let your mind be a pool of water. A pond without ripples."

Stink tried to pretend he was a pond. But how was being a pond going to help him with karate? Or thumb-wrestling? He told himself a joke instead. What do you call a pig that does karate? A pork chopper. Hardee-har-har.

"Silence, please," said Mr Albion.

Stink turned cherry-redder.

When they were done being pools of water, Sensei Dan showed Stink some hand positions.

"Remember, Stink: *karate* means *empty hand*." The only empty hand Stink cared about was the one for chopping bricks.

Next came a lot of standing around: horse stance, ready stance, cat stance. Standing was BOR-ing.

Standing was not kicking or punching or breaking stuff.

When Stink had to bow to Izzy, he head-butted her. When Stink had to bend like the willow, he fell over into a box of balls. And when Stink had to stand on one leg, a kid they called

Rooster Raymond said, "Dude. You look like a praying mantis."

At last, out came the punching bags! *Wham, slam, bam!* Stink Moody, aka Shark Hammersmash, was the Ultimate High-Flying, Punch-Bagging, Thumb-Wrestling Machine! On his way over to the Slammer, Stink tripped and tumbled into a forward roll.

"Hey, Ballerina Butt," Rooster hissed under his breath. "Dance class is next door."

"Mr Raymond." Sensei Dan pointed to a word over the mirror: RESPECT. "Don't make me remind you again."

Sensei Dan handed Stink a skipping-rope. "Mr Moody, how about if you step off the mat and do some work with the skipping-rope instead?"

Skipping-rope! You've got to be kidding! But Stink knew he had to respect the skipping-rope. At least until class was over.

When they were done, Stink asked, "Um, Mr Albion – I mean Sensei – I mean Dan, um, I was wondering, um, when is the karate-chopping?"

"Karate isn't just about the body, Mr Moody. It's about the mind too."

"Uh-huh."

"Many of my students have been practising a long time."

"Uh-huh."

"Karate is a discipline. A mindset. It doesn't just happen in a day."

"Uh-huh." Stink had his *mind set* on karate-chopping. Stink had his *mind set* on becoming the ultimate thumb-wrestling champ.

"Tell you what. Step on to the mat and I'll walk you through a side kick."

"Really? Thweet! I mean, sweet!"

"Stand on the blade of one foot. Bring your knee up and kick it out."

Shoom! Sensei Dan's left leg shot out, lightning fast.

"Maximum strike force!" yelled Stink. He punched the air, one-two.

"Now you try. Ready? Kick!"

Stink stood on one leg. Stink wobbled like a Weeble. Stink bent his knee and kicked! He spun around on one leg like a jewellery-box ballerina. His flying kick went flying. *Bam!* His left leg hit the cardboard Dragon Master right smack in the jaw. The Venerable Yuuto Kashiwagi crumpled to the ground. Stink landed on his butt. Again.

"Stink? Are you OK?"

"Are you kidding?" Stink asked. "Ka-rah-tay rocks!" New Guy Stink E. Moody, Ballerina Butt Boy, had just kicked the Dragon Master's butt!

Yarr!

Squawk!

LADIES AND GENTLEMEN!

THUMMY

VS

RAGIN' ROOSTER RAMSICLE

In this corner is Thummy. Straight from the crypt.

I'm gonna wrap you up, Rooster!

Up at dawn, ready to thumble, is the Rooster.

Is his crow worse than his throw?

I'm gonna cock-a-doodle crush you!

Cock-a-doodle -DON'T!

Thummy-Thummy Thumbster! Gonna toss ya in the Dumpster!

You're cracked. I'll make an omelette outta you.

WHACK!
THWACK!

Thummy the Mummy buries another one.

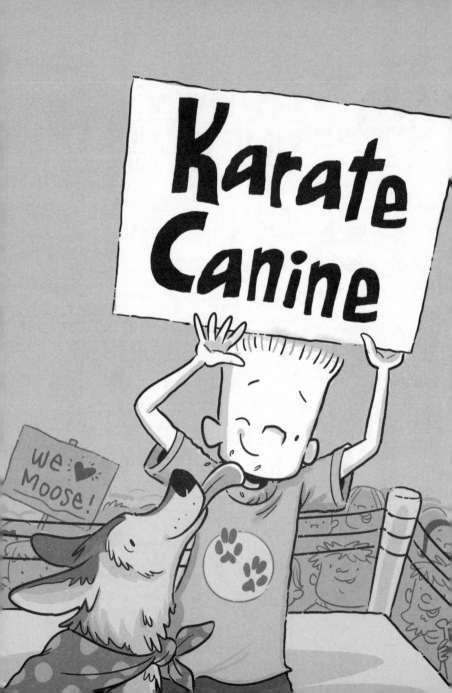

Stink got bitten by a bug. Not a bedbug. The karate bug! He practised kicks while Sophie did cartwheels. He practised stances when he wasn't thumb-wrestling Webster. He practised punches, even in the bathtub.

Stink planned to punch and kick his way to a yellow belt in just a few more weeks. And to celebrate, he was going to have a pizza party. An ultimate thumb-wrestling smackdown pizza party, that is.

Stink drank protein shakes. He ate energy bars. He dipped apple slices in peanut butter. Body *and* brain food.

When Sophie and Webster came over, Stink was pacing up and down the hall with library books on his head. He tried to memorize the karate Yellow Belt Creed. "I am only I. I come to you with only karate. Here are my empty hands, blah, blah, blah."

"How come you never want to do stuff any more?" Webster asked.

"Karate on the brain," said Sophie.

"*Karate* in the *body*," said Stink. The books tumbled to the ground.

"All I know is, you were way more fun before you became a sports freak."

"I can't stop now. I'm almost a yellow belt." Stink picked up his yellow belt list. "I know all my stances and a bunch of punches, and I have my side kick down. Plus I learned to respect the skipping-rope. If I can just learn the Yellow Belt Creed and—"

"*Harry the Dirty Dog*?" Sophie asked, picking up the books. "*Clifford the Big Red Dog*? *Go Dog Go*?"

"What's with all the baby books?" asked Webster.

"I thought you flunked gym, not reading," said Sophie.

"I'm going to read to a dog!" said Stink. "At the library. To get my yellow belt, I have to do three hours of community service."

"A *dog* in the *library*?" asked Sophie.

"They bring in dogs that are learning to be guide dogs, you know, to help blind people. But first the dog has to get used to people and kids and stuff."

"That's so bow-wow!" said Webster. "Can we come?"

101

Stink and his friends made a beeline for the library. "Is the reading dog here yet?"

"Any minute," said Lynn, the librarian.

At last! The dog that liked to read trotted into the library. Moose. He was a German shepherd with humongous ears and a pink tongue longer than a hot dog. *Slurp!* Moose licked Stink's whole face.

"Don't worry if you feel like an ice-cream cone," said Maggie, his trainer. "That's his way of getting to know you." In no time, the dog had turned Stink into a human Popsicle. "OK. I want Moose to get used to being around kids without me, so I'll be in the coffee shop out front."

Stink read a book about the big red dog at Halloween. Moose barked. "Maybe he's afraid of ghosts," said Webster.

Stink read the one where the big

red dog takes a bath. Moose yawned. "Maybe he doesn't like taking baths," said Sophie.

"I think that might be true," said Stink, pinching his nose.

Stink read the one about the big red dog and his first snow. Moose pricked up his ears. Stink turned the page. Stink turned another page. Moose rested his head on his paws.

"He likes it!" said Stink as Moose put his paw up on the book.

Sophie and Webster laughed. "Look! He's trying to turn the page!"

Stink chose a book about dog and

cat best friends. Moose grabbed the book and took off.

"Moose!" Stink called. "Come back here. Dogs can't read!" Stink chased after Moose. Webster and Sophie chased after Stink. Librarian Lynn chased after Webster and Sophie. They ran up and down rows of books. They chased Moose past mysteries, through cookbooks, to the corner where the U-Knitted Nations was having its Book Club meeting. Moose got all tangled up in a ball of blue wool. But did that stop him? No!

Rrrip! Moose leapt over the legs of a guy reading the paper. *Slurp!* He almost tipped over the table with the fish tank. *Crash!* He knocked over a trolley of kids' books.

"Horsey!" said a toddler, pointing.

Moose ran past her, heading straight for the front door.

"Stop! Moose!" Stink yelled. Moose ran right through the book detector. *Ree! Ree! Ree!* A siren louder than the Yack Buster went off. Moose stopped and turned.

"Be a good boy," Stink coaxed. "Give me back the library book."

Moose raced past Stink, almost knocking him over. He jumped into the book return bin – *Sproing!* Moose plopped down on a mountain of books.

"You just wanted to return your library book on time, huh, boy?"

"Arf!" said Moose. Stink reached for the book in Moose's mouth. *"Arf, arf, arf, arf, arf!"*

Stink remembered the willow. He made himself into a calm pool of water. He held out his empty hand towards Moose.

Moose dropped the book at last. By the time Maggie came back, Moose

had leapt into Stink's lap, licking his face. "Who's a reading dog? You are. Yes, you are," said Stink. "You should get your own Super Reading Award."

"And you should get an A+ in Community Service," said Maggie.

Moose lifted a paw in the air.

"Look! He's practising karate," said Stink. "He already knows horse stance!"

"Moose stance!" said Sophie, and they all cracked up.

Hiss!

LADIES AND GENTLEMEN!
THUMMY
VS.
THE DRAGON MASTER

Rrrr!

You're going down, Thummy!

Bring it!

Are you a dragon...

or a daisy?

Roar!
Slash!

Urg!

Crash!

Ha! Nice try.

I'm not fallin' for the old Snake in the Grass trick!

Thummy makes his move!

Time to wrap up this picnic!

Later

R.I.P. Dragon Master

Hee, hee, hee! Undefeated!

Saturday! Today was the day Stink would earn his yellow belt in karate!

By the time Stink got to Empty Hand Academy, he had jumping beans in his belly. He took in an ocean of deep breaths. He made himself still like a pool of water.

Judy, Mum and Dad sat at the back. Stink faced the mirror. *Mirror,*

mirror, on the wall, who's the yellow beltest of us all? Stink smiled. *Stop smiling! Focus! Concentrate!* Stink did not even tell himself a joke. He stood with three other kids and made his mind blank as a piece of paper.

Stink bowed to Sensei Dan. The room got dead quiet. *Hee-ya! Ai-ya! Ha! Ha! Ha!* Stink went through each stance. The audience clapped. Stink showed his skill with side kicks and roundhouse kicks. More clapping. He finished with a back-fist strike and punch.

Next, Stink sparred with Rooster. Then he handed in his community service paper. Last of all, Stink recited the Yellow Belt Creed. He bowed to Sensei Dan and waited for the panel of judges to call out names.

Ruby Yamamoto ... Rooster Raymond ... Stink Moody!

Sensei Dan held out the yellow belt. It was not blucky dirty like his old white belt. It was new and gold and shiny!

"When Stink first came to us, he was tripping over the mat," said Sensei Dan. "Now look at this young man. No one has worked harder these last few weeks. Stink Moody, on behalf of the Empty Hand Academy, it is with great honour that I bestow upon you this yellow belt. Wear it with respect and confidence."

✱ ✱ ✱

"Great job," said Dad.

"Rare," said Judy.

Stink wrapped the yellow belt around his waist twice. He knotted and unknotted his new belt, trying to get the ends even. "Sensei Dan says karate will help me with all sorts of stuff. I *so* don't stink at sports any more."

"But you so do stink at knots," said Judy.

"Do *not*. It's *not* as easy as you think to tie a reef *knot*," said Stink.

"You can play any sport you want, if you just put your mind to it," said Dad.

"So, you're a sports freak now, huh?" said Judy. "Too bad you didn't get a trophy."

Today, even big-sister Judy couldn't bug him. He looked down at his now-perfect knot. "But I got this cool uniform, and my yellow belt is kind of like a trophy, and now I get a pizza party! Right?"

"Right," said Dad.

"Right," said Mum.

"Can I have a thumb-wrestling pizza party at our house? And invite all my friends? For real? Can I wear my karate uniform too?"

"Maybe just this once," said Mum.

"Hi-ya!" Stink gave a spinning reverse punch in the air. "Take that,

old me who stinks at sports. There's a new kid on the block. Karate Stink. Just call me Yellow Belt Yeti."

Boo!

LADIES AND GENTLEMEN!
THUMMY
VS.
THE THUMB-SUCKER

EEE!

Round 1

Hey, Binky Boo-hoo, come out from under your blankie!

BOO!

AAAGH!

Round 2 Thummy moves in for the final put-down.

Nanny, nanny, boo-hoo! Don't be such a yoo-hoo!

Whirl!

Time to unwrap the mummy!

Who wants their mummy now?

At last it was time. Time for the smackdown at Stink Moody's house. The Ultimate Thumb-Wrestling *Thmack*down.

Stink could hardly wait to thumb-wrestle. This time, he had a not-so-secret secret weapon. Karate!

Stink put on his karate uniform and headband. Stink tied his yellow belt in a perfect reef knot. Stink wore his lucky shark tooth around his neck.

"Shark Hammersmash, you and me are gonna be the ultimate thumb-wrestling champs of the world."

The back garden was full of kids thumb-wrestling. Webster, Sophie and Skunk. Ruby and Rooster. Heather Strong. Riley Rottenberger.

"Stink!"

"Finally!"

"Where were you?"

"What took you so long?"

"I already crushed Skunk. And that guy Rooster," said Webster. "Stink. You gotta play me. If I beat you, T. Rex will be undefeated."

Stink stood across from Webster. Stink swallowed. Stink checked the knot in his belt. It was about the size of the knot in his stomach. But Stink would stare down that knot. He would become a pool of water.

Skunk stood on an upside-down rubbish bin. *Ding! Ding! Ding!* He yelled into a ketchup-bottle microphone. "Hey, sports fans! Get ready for the final match of the Ultimate Thumb-Wrestling Thmackdown. On the left, we have T. Rex Wasabi. He's strong. He's sneaky. He's the Superman of Thumb-Wrestling. He's already smacked down six wrestlers. Will T. Rex Wasabi go undefeated?"

"No way!"

"Way!"

"T. Rex is dust! The Shark rules!"

"T. Rex rules more!"

"And on the right, we have underdog Shark Hammersmash. He may be shrimpy, but he's as mighty as a great white. Slippery, too."

Bend like the willow. Be still like the pond. Stink did not feel like a pond. His belly felt like an ocean full of crashing waves.

"Knuckle up, boys," called Skunk. "Ready to rumble?"

Webster slipped on his T. Rex Wasabi mask. Stink checked the Shark on his thumb. He rubbed his shark tooth for good luck.

"Let's bow to each other with our thumbs." The Shark bowed to T. Rex, just like in karate. T. Rex did the same.

"Lock 'em up and smash 'em down," called Skunk, punching the air.

Webster dipped and ducked his thumb back and forth, up, down and sideways, tempting Stink to go for a slam.

"Body slam! T. Rex almost makes sushi out of the Shark," yelled Skunk.

Stink slid his thumb out from under Webster's. "But the Shark is slippery."

I am strong like the willow, Stink thought. *I am mighty like the oak. I am swift like the tiger. I am slippery like the eel.*

"Head-butt!" called Skunk.

"Crush 'em, T. Rex!"

"C'mon, Shark. Don't be a Thumbelina!"

Focus. Be a blank piece of paper.

"Oh no! T. Rex came out of nowhere and pinned the Shark! One, two—"

T. Rex had a stranglehold on him. Stink slipped his thumb out in the nick of time. "And he's back!" yelled Skunk.

"He's a slippery one. The Electric Eel."

"Hammer him, Shark!"

"Bite back, T. Rex!" the kids yelled.

Stink was huffing. Webster was puffing. Stink was sweating. Webster's glasses slid down his nose.

"Give up?" Webster asked Stink.

Never give up, Stink heard Sensei Dan say. So far, the Shark had survived two standoffs, one face-off and one almost-smackdown. He had sidestepped a Snake in the Grass, a Santa's Little Helper and a Tsunami Smash. And he'd come back from a Banana Split. "No way! Do you give up?"

"Never," said Webster.

"TIME!" called Sophie. But Stink did not stop. Stink kept on dipping, ducking and dodging. Webster kept sneaking in for a sideways slam.

Stink was the Electric Eel in a pool of water. He was as strong as a willow. He would not break. He was a crouching tiger, ready to pounce.

Out of nowhere, Stink made a way-tricky lightning-fast move. Shark Hammersmash flew off his thumb.

"One, two, three!" Stink pinned Webster for three counts. At last, Shark Hammersmash had taken down the mighty T. Rex with his bare thumb. Stink had played his best game ever. Thumbs down.

"Good match, T. Rex," said Stink.

"Great match! I never even saw you coming. What *was* that? A double-reverse Snake in the Grass? An upside-down sideways Tsunami Smash?"

"Just a little move I made up called Crouching Tiger, Hidden Thumb."

"Wow!" said Webster. "You should enter the Thumb-Wrestling Olympics or something. You could get into the Thumb-Wrestling Hall of Fame with that move!"

Skunk held out the ketchup-bottle microphone. "So, Shark Hammersmash, you, and you alone, took down the mighty T. Rex. Tell us sports fans out here. How do you feel?"

"Absolutely, positively, thumb-tastic!" said Stink.

10 Things You May Not Know About Megan McDonald

10. The first story Megan ever got published (in the fifth grade) was about a pencil sharpener.

9. She read the biography of Virginia Dare so many times at her school library that the librarian had to ask her to give somebody else a chance.

8. She had to be a boring-old pilgrim every year for Halloween because she has four older sisters, who kept passing their pilgrim costumes down to her.

7. Her favourite board game is the Game of Life.

6. She is a member of the Ice-Cream-for-Life Club at Screamin' Mimi's in her hometown of Sebastopol, California.

5. She has a Band-Aid collection to rival Judy Moody's, including bacon-scented Band-Aids.

4. She owns a jawbreaker that is bigger than a baseball, which she will never, ever eat.

3. Like Stink, she had a pet newt that slipped down the drain when she was his age.

2. She often starts a book by scribbling on a napkin.

1. And the number-one thing you may not know about Megan McDonald is: she was once the opening act for the World's Biggest Cupcake!

10 Things You May Not Know About Peter H. Reynolds

10. He has a twin brother, Paul. Paul was born first, fourteen minutes before Peter decided to arrive.

9. Peter is part owner of a children's book and toy shop called the Blue Bunny in the Massachusetts town where he lives.

8. He's vertically challenged (aka short!).

7. His mother is from England; his father is from Argentina.

6. He made his first animated film while he was in high school.

5. He sometimes paints with tea instead of water – whatever's handy!

4. He keeps a sketch pad and pen on his nightstand. That way, if an idea hits him in the middle of the night, he can jot it down immediately.

3. His favourite candy is a tie between peanut-butter cups and chocolate-covered raisins (same as Megan McDonald!).

2. One of his favourite books growing up was *The Tall Book of Make-Believe* by Jane Werner, illustrated by Garth Williams.

1. And the number-one thing you may not know about Peter H. Reynolds is: he shares a birthday with James Madison, Stink's favourite president!

Be sure to check out more Stink adventures!

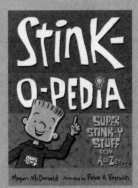

Judy Moody and Stink are starring together!

Judy Moody and Stink
The Holly Joliday

Judy Moody and Stink
The Mad, Mad, Mad, Mad
Treasure Hunt

In full color

Need more Moody? Try These!

Stink

has his own super website!

www.stinkmoody.com

Go online to:

- Make your own comics.

- Host your own Way-Official Moody Stink-a-thon.

- Help Astro with a guinea pig maze.

- Read exclusive excerpts from Stink's books.

- Find lots of new Stink-y information and activities!